For my kids. I love you forever.

Come on, let's go practice !"

Every day, Charliana and Alexiana practiced their dancing. They loved to tap dance very much and practiced as much as they could.

They loved it so much that their parents made them a practice space in the basement. They kept all their dance shoes there and even had a huge mirror to see themselves when they danced.

Even though it was in the basement and very cold, the practice room was their favorite place to be in the house.

But one day, they started to notice that the room was different. Usually, they left the room neat, but that began to change.

From that day on, it was always a bit different when they went into it. The sound system would be turned to a very low volume. The girls' shoes would be moved ever so slightly.

The biggest (or smallest) difference they noticed was that there was a tiny pair of tap shoes left in the middle of the floor each night.

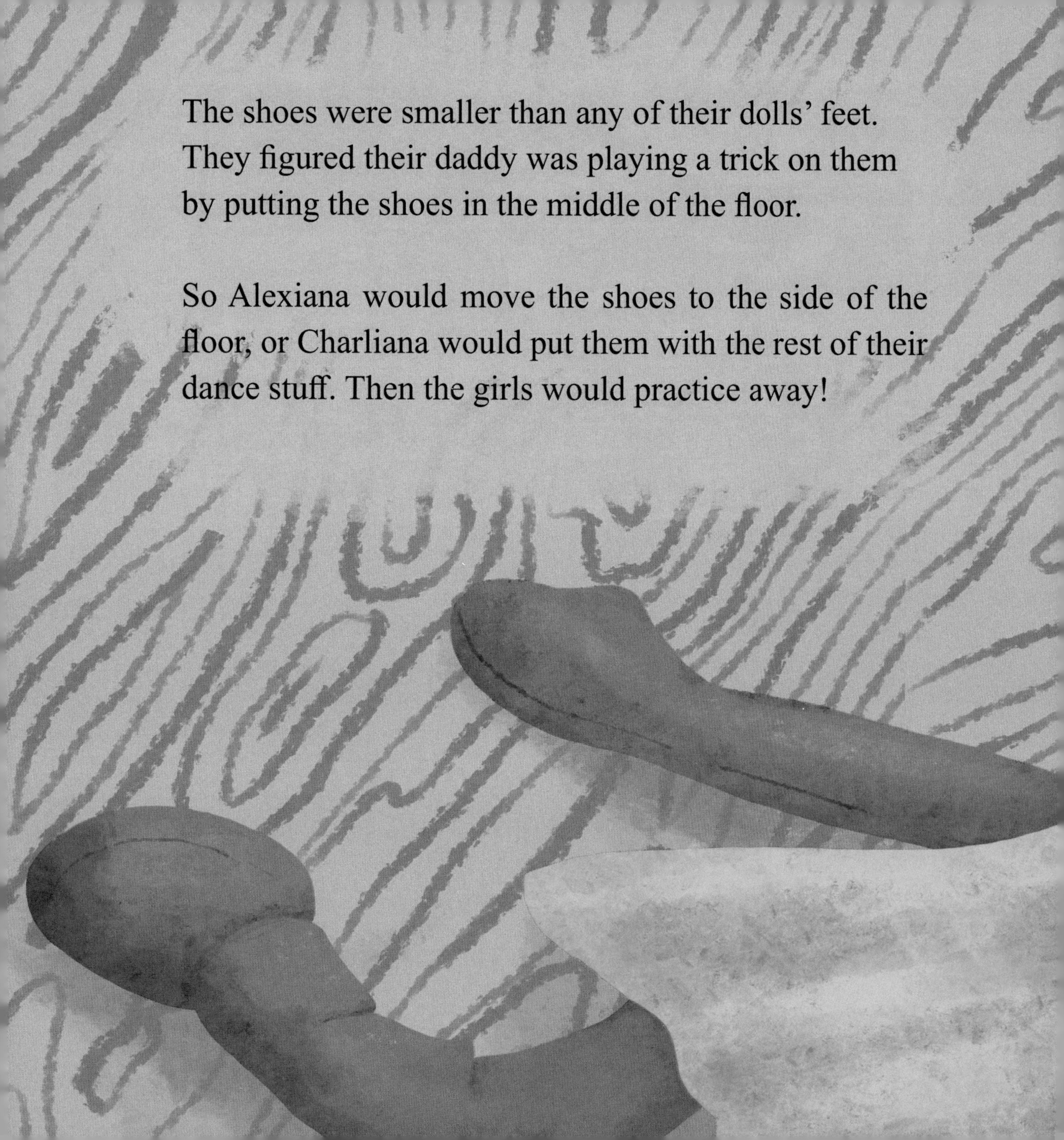

The shoes were smaller than any of their dolls' feet. They figured their daddy was playing a trick on them by putting the shoes in the middle of the floor.

So Alexiana would move the shoes to the side of the floor, or Charliana would put them with the rest of their dance stuff. Then the girls would practice away!

In the mornings before everyone woke up, their daddy would go into the practice room to make sure the switches were turned off and things put away.

And every morning, he'd see those tiny tap shoes and wonder why the girls left them in the room.

Often, he'd take the tiny tap shoes and put them in the girls' toy bin with the rest of their dolls' dress-up clothes. Other times, he'd move them to the shoe bin. He was always wondering why the shoes were important to his daughters.

Late at night, or whenever the house was quiet, a little light would appear at the girls' window.

It was Steve the Fairy! He lived in the ice cream cone on top of a local ice cream shop called Inside Scoop.

He felt love and warmth in the house where the two girls lived. So he started visiting the family often, sometimes two or three times a day.

He loved the music and dance that he found there and would go inside and dance in the practice room every day.

First, he would have to find the place where the girls had hidden his tap shoes each day. It was a fun game they played with him.

He'd fly around the house until he found them.

He would then put his shoes on and dance away.

After long hours of practice, Steve would take his shoes off in the middle of the floor and fly up to the parents' room. He would sprinkle a little forgetful fairy dust on the mommy and daddy in case they heard him, and he would sprinkle some happy fairy dust on the girls because they inspired him.

All of his practice was for the Fairy Ball that was scheduled in two weeks. Steve was going to show everyone his tap dancing. He loved tap very much and was incredibly happy that he was going to show all his friends his love of dance at this special party.

The next day, something went wrong. The girls practiced. The parents cleaned up. But on this night, the mommy took the shoes out of the studio and brought them to her bedroom.

She set them on the nightstand next to the daddy's phone and went to take a shower. When the daddy came to the room and picked up his phone, he knocked the tiny shoes off the nightstand and into the trash!!

That night, Steve the Fairy showed up to practice. He flew into the practice space, but his shoes were gone!

He looked everywhere for them.

He looked in the shoe bin, in the dollhouse. He looked around the studio and in the refrigerator; he even looked in the bathroom toilet!

No shoes. Steve was so sad.

He decided to practice a little without tap shoes on, but it just wasn't the same.

He knew he had only one choice: he needed to show Charliana and Alexiana that he existed.

Steve sat at the foot of Alexiana's bed. He threw some sunshine fairy dust into the air, and the room lit up like a warm summer morning. Alexiana rubbed her eyes as she opened them.

Steve flew to her and landed on her nose so that she wouldn't miss him and said, "Hi!"

Alexiana screamed and jumped out of the bed. "A fairy!" Steve tried to quiet her down, but Charliana woke up to the noises asking, "Where?!" from the other room.

"Right there! Right there!" Alexiana yelled as Charliana came running into her room. When she saw Steve, she ran right into the wall, she was so surprised.

Their mommy walked in and asked, "What is all the excitement about?"

Then their daddy walked in. Steve was hiding behind a few pieces of popcorn. He decided he could just appear to the whole family and sprinkle forgetful fairy dust on them. So he came out.

"WOW!" the whole family said. A real fairy.

Steve said to the family, “I’m very sorry to bother you all, but my tap shoes are missing!”

Mommy replied, “Oh, those were yours! I brought them to my room last night to show Daddy.” She turned to Daddy and asked, “Did you see them? They were next to your phone.”

Daddy said, “No. I came in last night, checked my phone, and went to bed.”

They all ran down the hall (except Steve, who flew) to see if the shoes were still there. They looked everywhere: under the bed, in the sheets, even in Daddy’s slippers. But they were nowhere to be found.

Mommy asked, "Could they have fallen off of the nightstand and into the trash?"

Daddy said, "Today is trash day. I took the trash out first thing."

Just then, they heard the trash truck!

Steve said, "My shoes must be in there! If I don't dance at the ball, I won't be able to make everyone smile and share in my joy of dance. I am the featured performer this year, for the first time. We need to get them!"

They all ran outside and started chasing after the truck. Alexiana scooped up Steve and put him in her pocket.

Charliana jumped on her bike.

Alexiana sat behind her, putting her arms around her waist, and they were off.

The truck was about to get on the highway. If it did that, there was no way they could catch it, and the shoes would be in the dump—lost forever.

Steve said, “Throw me! I can make it to the truck!”

So Alexiana threw Steve as hard as she could, and he went soaring through the air, finally landing on the truck. He ran across the top, tripped and fell over the front of the truck, and got stuck to the windshield like a smushed bug.

"Stop, please!" he yelled.

The truck driver was shocked and slammed on the breaks, pulling over just before he got on the highway, then got out just as the girls caught up to him. He looked everywhere for the giant bug (or little fairy) that was on his windshield. Steve flew away from the driver never to be seen by him again. The girls told the driver that they had dropped an important keepsake in the trash and really wanted to look for it.

The driver told them, "It's really stinky in there, but okay. Don't tell anyone I let you do this."

The girls were about to jump into the back to find the shoes, but Steve was inside already and had found them. The girls turned to the driver after seeing Steve and said,
"On second thought, you're right. It's too stinky to look in there."

"We are sorry to waste your time." Meanwhile, Steve was sprinkling forgetful fairy dust on the driver.

After he did, the driver asked, "Why did I stop here? Hmmm, I better get to the dump. Have a great day, ladies."

Back at home, everyone was exhausted. What an exciting day! They noted that they had a visiting fairy in their house every night. What a lucky house we have, they thought to themselves.

Steve said to them, “I really should make you all forget, in order to keep myself and my friends safe.”

Daddy replied, “We understand. Come visit anytime.”

Steve thought for a moment; then he pulled out truthful fairy dust and sprinkled it over the family.

“Can you keep my secret?’ They all said “yes!” He knew he could trust them!

He waved to them all, and he flew away.

The next day, the father said, “Girls, have you practiced today?”

“Heading down now.”

The girls went back to their daily practice routine. But now they had a special guest. They helped Steve to get ready for his performance. They wished they could join him and meet all the fairies. But they knew they were fortunate to know this one very special fairy.

When he finished, he said

“I could never have done it without all of you and my two special friends. They know who they are!”

Made in the USA
Middletown, DE
19 December 2021